Giants and Wild, Hairy Monsters

by Janet Perry and Victor Gentle

To Lena, the Wild Monster from Whitefish Bay

Gareth Stevens Publishing
MILWAUKEE

For a free color catalog describing Gareth Stevens' list of high-quality books and multimedia programs, call 1-800-542-2595 (USA) or 1-800-461-9120 (Canada). Gareth Stevens Publishing's Fax: (414) 225-0377.

Library of Congress Cataloging-in-Publication Data

Perry, Janet, 1960-
    Giants and wild, hairy monsters / by Janet Perry and Victor Gentle.
      p. cm. — (Monsters: an imagination library series)
    Includes bibliographical references (p. 22) and index.
    Summary: Examines the existence of mythical and fictional monsters that are big and hairy, including King Kong, the Abominable Snowman, and Sasquatch.
    ISBN 0-8368-2437-7 (lib. bdg.)
    1. Giants—Juvenile literature. 2. Monsters—Juvenile literature.
[1. Giants. 2. Monsters.] I. Gentle, Victor. II. Title. III. Series: Perry, Janet, 1960- Monsters.
GR560.P47   1999
001.9—dc21   99-14719

First published in 1999 by
Gareth Stevens Publishing
1555 North RiverCenter Drive, Suite 201
Milwaukee, WI 53212 USA

Text: Janet Perry and Victor Gentle
Page layout: Janet Perry, Victor Gentle, and Helene Feider
Cover design: Joel Bucaro and Helene Feider
Series editor: Patricia Lantier-Sampon
Editorial assistant: Diane Laska

Photo credits: Cover, pp. 5, 7, 9, 11 © Photofest; p. 13 © Russell D. Curtis/Photo Researchers, Inc.; pp. 15, 17 © Popperfoto/Archive Photos; p. 19 Wisconsin Center for Film and Theater Research, University of Wisconsin-Madison; p. 21 © Warner Bros./Archive Photos

Printed in the United States of America

1 2 3 4 5 6 7 8 9 03 02 01 00 99

Front cover: In *King Kong* (1976), Kong has Dwan right in the palm of his hand. His heart is wrapped around her little finger — too bad she fears heights!

TABLE OF CONTENTS

Words that appear in the glossary are printed in **boldface**
type the first time they occur in the text.

THUD!

THUD! THUD! THUD! Great oak trees crash to Earth. The concrete heaves and crumbles. The ground is *rippling* under your feet. Something very big is walking in your direction.

Do you turn to stare, and risk getting flattened like the silly people in movies? Will you stick around and try to identify this monster as it raises a massive foot and blots out the sun?

THUD! **THUD! THUD! THUD!**

No way! Don't walk — *RUN! HIDE!*

He's as tall as a building and as heavy as a truck, and now he's mad! If I were you, I wouldn't monkey with King Kong.

A HAIRY, GENTLE, WILD, FEROCIOUS THING!!??

King Kong is a movie about Kong, a **giant** ape that is kidnapped from his island home and taken to New York City to be a sideshow freak.

On his island, he's worshiped as a god. In New York City, he's a prisoner in chains. When he tries to escape, people shoot at him, buzz him with helicopters, and send the army to kill him. This scares Kong, and he becomes angry. Wouldn't you be scared and angry, too?

Yet, he's always gentle to Dwan, an actress who was given to him as a human sacrifice. He's certainly monster-sized, but is he a monster at heart?

Kong's an island boy, too wild for civilization. He can escape, but he can't hide. A king-sized ape stands out — wherever he goes!

NOT JUST ANOTHER PRETTY FACE

You might wish that you were bigger, sometimes, just so people would notice you.

In the movie *Attack of the 50 Foot Woman*, Nancy Fowler is ignored by everyone. Then she meets an alien that zaps her with a growth ray.

The giant Nancy sets out for revenge on her husband, Harry, and on everyone else who had made her feel so small. *Now* they are going to notice her. She crushes cars, smashes a building, and strides through town yelling, "Har-ry! Har-ry!"

If people had paid attention to her report of an alien invasion, Nancy never would have had her . . . big break . . . in this 1958 movie.

GOING UP!

Real people who are giants were not zapped by aliens testing growth rays on humans. They were born that way.

Your body produces a special substance called **somatotrophin,** or **growth hormone**. Depending on how much growth hormone your body produces, it may grow larger or smaller than another person's body. Most people produce hormones within a certain range, which we call "normal."

A few people have much more growth hormone than others do — far beyond the normal range! Those people might grow to be almost 9 feet (2.7 meters) tall. This is called **gigantism**.

Richard Kiel plays "Jaws" in a scene from *Moonraker* (1979). As he grabs James Bond, you can see Mr. Kiel is unusually tall. Do you think he has gigantism?

GROWING, GROWING, GROWN

Giant is a **relative** word. A "giant" tomato is bigger than the biggest normal tomato. But it is smaller than a normal watermelon.

When vegetables and fish grow to be humongous, gigantism is not the cause. Like humans, these **organisms** have hormones that tell them to grow as big as they possibly can, as long as they have enough food, water, light, and heat.

Just because some people are unusually big, they don't necessarily have gigantism. They are just naturally big.

Some pumpkins grow to be massive when given the right stuff. They seem gigantic only because we don't usually see pumpkins so big.

FOSSIL PUZZLES AND FOOTPRINT HINTS

Before **paleontology** was established as a science, it was difficult to identify some of the large, **fossilized** bones people came across. The bones often did not match those of animals they knew. Sometimes, the fossils were too strange — or were just very big. People didn't know then that some of these fossils belonged to extinct animals.

So, the bones were a puzzle. One answer that seemed to fit was that somewhere, hiding deep in the forests or high in the mountains, there were giants — giant animals or giant people.

Strange bones were not the only mysteries. This 1951 photo was taken high in the mountains in Nepal. What could have made this giant footprint?

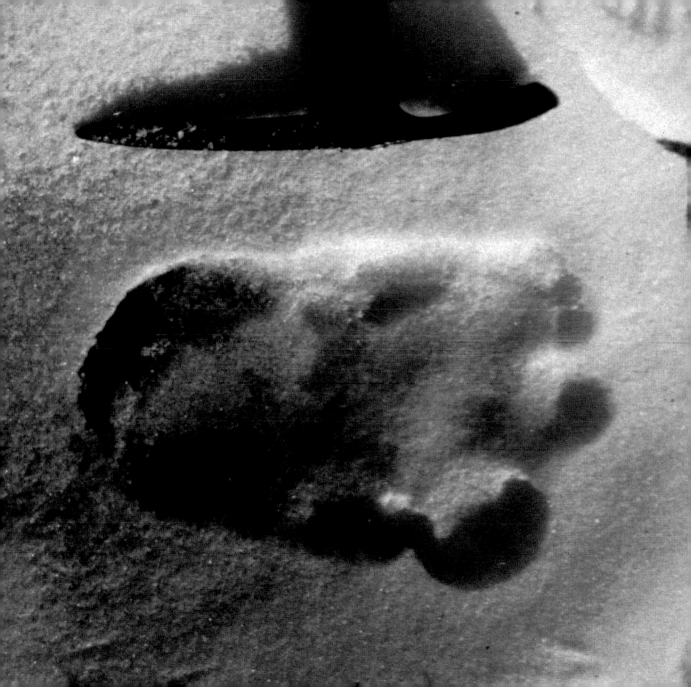

SURVIVORS FROM ANOTHER AGE?

History and myth are filled with marvelous stories of large, wild, humanlike creatures wandering in the wilderness.

Many reports said these creatures were taller than humans, with **conical** skulls, apelike faces, prominent teeth, and furry bodies. We still hear of sightings like this today. It is not so hard to picture these creatures, still hiding in the remaining wild places on our planet.

Many of the creatures reported were probably just bears, apes, or even **feral** humans (people who were left in the wild from childhood, and survived). But were some of them . . . something else?

Some sightings may be **hoaxes** or jokes. This is an image from a 1973 video taken in Spokane, Washington. Experts say it's a fake.

THOSE WILD, HAIRY ONES

People who saw apelike creatures during medieval times tried to talk to them. The creatures replied in grunts and snarls. They did not use tools, nor did they know how to make fire.

Civilized people called them "wild, hairy ones." They are known by different names all over the world. Dwellers of the Himalayan Mountains call them yeti, and Russians call them almas. Native American names for them are Sasquatch and Oh-Mah. Other North Americans may call them Bigfoot, Jack-O, or the abominable snowman.

Their existence has never been proved, but they *might* be real.

That about wraps it up for this wild, hairy one. He's laid out cold in the movie *The Abominable Snowman of the Himalayas* (1957). But what about that photo on page 15?

IS THE TRUTH OUT THERE, HAIRY BUT HIDDEN?

Many kinds of animals have been discovered only in the last 200 years — including some big ones.

The giant panda has lived in China since before the Ice Age. It was only "officially" discovered by a French explorer in 1869! "Unofficial" stories of giant pandas were told by villagers and travelers for many years before that.

Stories of wild, hairy ones have been around a long time, too. So, it's possible that they are just very good at hiding.

Even so, they are probably quite different from the wild imaginings of moviemakers.

Dr. Brockton examines a troglodyte in the 1970 movie *Trog.* She tries to talk with it, thinking it may be a link to humans of the past.

MORE TO READ, VIEW, AND LISTEN TO

Books (Nonfiction)

America's Very Own Monsters. Daniel Cohen (Dodd, Mead)
Beastly Tales: Yeti, Bigfoot and the Loch Ness Monster.
  Malcolm Yorke (DK)
Beasts. Stewart Ross (Copper Beech)
The Living World. Record Breakers (series). David Lambert
  (Gareth Stevens)
Monsters. Bernard Brett (Wanderer)
Monsters (series). Janet Perry and Victor Gentle (Gareth Stevens)
The Sasquatch. Roland Smith (Hyperion)
Science Looks at Mysterious Monsters. Thomas G. Aylesworth
  (Messner)

Books (Activity)

Dragons and Prehistoric Monsters. Draw, Model, and Paint (series).
  Isidro Sánchez (Gareth Stevens)
Let's All Draw Monsters, Ghosts, Ghouls, and Demons.
  Jane Robertson (Watson-Guptil)
Monster Jokes. Diane Dow Suire (Children's Press)

Books (Fiction)

Dragon, Dragon, and Other Tales. John Gardner (Knopf)
Making Friends with Frankenstein. Colin McNaughton (Candlewick)
Monster Soup and Other Spooky Poems. Dilys Evans (Scholastic)
13 Monsters Who Should Be Avoided. Kevin Shortsleeve (Peachtree)

Videos (Fiction)

The Abominable Snowman of the Himalayas.
  (Hammer Films/20th Century Fox)
Attack of the 50 Foot Woman. (Warner)
BFG Big Friendly Giant. (Celebrity)
The Giant of Thunder Mountain. (Plaza)
Jack the Giant Killer. (MGM/UA Studios)
King Kong. (Paramount)

WEB SITES

If you have your own computer and Internet access, great! If not, most libraries have Internet access. Go to your library and enter the word *museums* into the library's preferred search engine. See if you can find a museum web page that has exhibits on fossils, the Himalayas, Neanderthals, or Roman myths about feral children. If any of these museums are close by, you can visit them in person!

The Internet changes every day, and web sites come and go. We believe the sites we recommend here are likely to last, and give the best and most appropriate links for our readers to pursue their interest in folklore and facts about extra-large people who lived in the past and who might live with us now.

www.ajkids.com

This is the junior *Ask Jeeves* site – it's a great research tool.

Some questions to try out in *Ask Jeeves Kids*:
- *Where can I find information about real giants?*
- *Who is the tallest woman in the world?*
- *Where is the Cardiff Giant?*
- *How do hormones work?*

You can also just type in words and phrases with "?" at the end, for example,
- *Attack of the 50 Foot Woman?*
- *Gigantism?*

www.mzoo.com

The Miniature Zoo has a special section of monsters and weird critters. Go to the site and click on the Quick Site Index to see pictures and links to many strange and unusual beasties of myth and legend, including apelike human critters that wander the Earth!

www.yahooligans.com

This is the junior Yahoo! home page. Click on one of the listed topics (such as Around the World, Science and Nature) for more links. From Around the World, try Anthropology and Archaeology and Mythology and Folklore to find more sites on giants. From Science and Nature, you might try Dinosaurs, Animals, Living Things, or Museums and Exhibits to find out more about fossils, gigantism, and extra-large people in the circus and in movies. You can also search for more information by typing a word in the Yahooligans search engine. Some words to try are: *Big Foot, Cardiff Giant, giant, missing link, Sasquatch,* and *troglodyte.*

GLOSSARY

You can find these words on the pages listed. Reading a word in a sentence helps you understand it even better.

conical (KON-ih-kul) — pointy; conelike 16

feral (FEAR-uhl) — living in the wild like a wild animal 16

fossilized — hardened inside a rock; if the remains of an animal or plant are fossilized, they become hard, encased in rock that forms around them over thousands of years 14

giant — much bigger than normal 6, 8, 12, 14, 20

gigantism (jye-GAN-tizm) — a medical condition where the body makes too much of the substance that controls growth, causing extra-tall or extra-large people 10, 12

growth hormone — a special substance, such as **somatotrophin**, that our bodies produce to control how big we grow 10

hoaxes (HOAKS-iz) — tricks people use to get other people to believe what isn't true 16

organisms (OR-guhn-IH-zumz) — living animals or plants 12

paleontology (PAY-lee-uhn-TAHL-oh-gee) — the scientific study of fossilized remains from ancient periods in Earth's history 14

relative — used for comparison; for example, relative to a tiger, a cat is small, but relative to a mouse, it is big 12

INDEX